POLE
BIG STONES AND ROX
BEE TREE
RABBITS FRENDS AND RALETIONS
MY HOUSE
OWLS HOUSE
100 AKER WOOD
EEYORES GLOOMY PLACE
RATHER BOGGY AND SAD

STORIES OF WINNIE-THE-POOH BY A A MILNE

together with favourite poems

with original illustrations by Ernest H Shepard

Published in 1992 by Dean,
in association with Methuen Children's Books
an imprint of Egmont Children's Books Limited
239 Kensington High Street, London W8 6SA
This version published in 2000 for Index Books Ltd.
Printed and bound in China

ISBN 0 603 56012 1

1 3 5 7 9 10 8 6 4 2

Contents

IN WHICH WE ARE INTRODUCED TO WINNIE-THE-POOH AND SOME BEES, AND THE STORIES BEGIN

Here is Edward Bear, coming downstairs now, bump, bump, bump, on the back of his head, behind Christopher Robin. It is, as far as he knows, the only way of coming downstairs, but sometimes he feels that there really is another way, if only he could stop bumping for a moment and think of it. And then he feels that perhaps there isn't. Anyhow, here he is at the bottom, and ready to be introduced to you. Winnie-the-Pooh.

When I first heard his name, I said, just as you are going to say, "But I thought he was a boy?"

"So did I," said Christopher Robin.

"Then you can't call him Winnie?"

"I don't."

"But you said —"

"He's Winnie-ther-Pooh. Don't you know what '*ther*' means?"

"Ah, yes, now I do," I said quickly; and I hope you do too, because it is all the explanation you are going to get.

Sometimes Winnie-the-Pooh likes a game of some sort when he comes downstairs, and sometimes he likes to sit quietly in front of the fire and listen to a story. This evening —

"What about a story?" said Christopher Robin.

"*What* about a story?" I said.

"Could you very sweetly tell Winnie-the-Pooh one?"

"I suppose I could," I said. "What sort of stories does he like?"

"About himself. Because he's *that* sort of Bear."

"Oh, I see."

"So could you very sweetly?"

"I'll try," I said.

So I tried.

• • • • •

Once upon a time, a very long time ago now, about last Friday, Winnie-the-Pooh lived in a forest all by himself under the name of Sanders.

("*What does 'under the name' mean?*" *asked Christopher Robin.*

"*It means he had the name over the door in gold letters and lived under it.*"

"Winnie-the-Pooh wasn't quite sure," said Christopher Robin.
"Now I am," said a growly voice.
"Then I will go on," said I.)

One day when he was out walking, he came to an open place in the middle of the forest, and in the middle of this place was a large oak-tree, and, from the top of the tree, there came a loud buzzing-noise.

Winnie-the-Pooh sat down at the foot of the tree, put his head between his paws, and began to think.

First of all he said to himself: "That buzzing-noise means something. You don't get a buzzing-noise like that, just buzzing and buzzing, without its meaning something. If there's a buzzing-noise, somebody's making a buzzing-noise, and the only reason for making a buzzing-noise that *I* know of is because you're a bee."

Then he thought another long time, and said: "And the only reason for being a bee that I know of is making honey."

And then he got up, and said: "And the only reason for making honey is so as *I* can eat it." So he began to climb the tree.

He climbed and he climbed and he climbed, and as he climbed he sang a little song to himself. It went like this:

Isn't it funny
How a bear likes honey?
Buzz! Buzz! Buzz!
I wonder why he does?

Then he climbed a little further . . . and a little further . . . and then just a little further. By that time he had thought of another song.

It's a very funny thought that, if Bears were Bees,
They'd build their nests at the bottom *of trees.*
And that being so (if the Bees were Bears),
We shouldn't have to climb up all these stairs.

He was getting rather tired by this time, so that is why he sang a Complaining Song. He was nearly there now, and if he just stood on that branch . . .

Crack!

"Oh, help!" said Pooh, as he dropped ten feet on the branch below him.

"If only I hadn't —" he said, as he bounced twenty feet on to the next branch.

"You see, what I *meant* to do," he explained, as he turned head-over-heels, and crashed on to another branch thirty feet below, "what I *meant* to do —"

"Of course, it *was* rather —" he admitted, as he slithered very quickly through the next six branches.

"It all comes, I suppose," he decided, as he said good-bye to the last branch, spun round three times, and flew gracefully into a gorse-bush, "it all comes of *liking* honey so much. Oh, help!"

He crawled out of the gorse-bush, brushed the prickles from his nose, and began to think again. And the first person he thought of was Christopher Robin.

("Was that me?" said Christopher Robin in an awed voice, hardly daring to believe it.

"That was you."

Christopher Robin said nothing, but his eyes got larger and larger, and his face got pinker and pinker.)

So Winnie-the-Pooh went round to his friend Christopher Robin, who lived behind a green door in another part of the Forest.

"Good morning, Christopher Robin," he said.

"Good morning, Winnie-*ther*-Pooh," said you.

"I wonder if you've got such a thing as a balloon about you?"

"A balloon?"

"Yes, I just said to myself coming along: 'I wonder if Christopher Robin has such a thing as a balloon about him?'

I just said it to myself, thinking of balloons, and wondering."

"What do you want a balloon for?" you said.

Winnie-the-Pooh looked round to see that nobody was listening, put his paw to his mouth, and said in a deep whisper: "*Honey!*"

"But you don't get honey with balloons!"

"*I* do," said Pooh.

Well, it just happened that you had been to a party the day before at the house of your friend Piglet, and you had balloons at the party. You had had a big green balloon; and one of

Rabbit's relations had had a big blue one, and had left it behind, being really too young to go to a party at all; and so you had brought the green one *and* the blue one home with you.

"Which one would you like?" you asked Pooh.

He put his head between his paws and thought very carefully.

"It's like this," he said. "When you go after honey with a balloon, the great thing is not to let the bees know you're coming. Now, if you have a green balloon, they might think you were only part of the tree, and not notice you, and if you

have a blue balloon, they might think you were only part of the sky, and not notice you, and the question is: Which is most likely?"

"Wouldn't they notice *you* underneath the balloon?" you asked.

"They might or they might not," said Winnie-the-Pooh. "You never can tell with bees." He thought for a moment and said: "I shall try to look like a small black cloud. That will deceive them."

"Then you had better have the blue balloon," you said; and so it was decided.

Well, you both went out with the blue balloon, and you took your gun with you, just in case, as you always did, and Winnie-the-Pooh went to a very muddy place that he knew of, and rolled and rolled until he was black all over; and then,

when the balloon was blown up as big as big, and you and Pooh were both holding on to the string, you let go suddenly, and Pooh Bear floated gracefully up into the sky, and stayed there — level with the top of the tree and about twenty feet away from it.

"Hooray!" you shouted.

"Isn't that fine?" shouted Winnie-the-Pooh down to you. "What do I look like?"

"You look like a Bear holding on to a balloon," you said.

"Not," said Pooh anxiously, "— not like a small black cloud in a blue sky?"

"Not very much."

"Ah, well, perhaps from up here it looks different. And, as I say, you never can tell with bees."

There was no wind to blow him nearer to the tree so there he stayed. He could see the honey, he could smell the honey, but he couldn't quite reach the honey.

After a little while he called down to you.

"Christopher Robin!" he said in a loud whisper.

"Hallo!"

"I think the bees *suspect* something!"

"What sort of thing?"

"I don't know. But something tells me that they're *suspicious*!"

"Perhaps they think that you're after their honey?"

"It may be that. You never can tell with bees."

There was another little silence, and then he called down to you again.

"Christopher Robin!"

"Yes?"

"Have you an umbrella in your house?"

"I think so."

"I wish you would bring it out here, and walk up and down with it, and look up at me every now and then, and say 'Tut-tut, it looks like rain.' I think, if you did that, it would help the deception which we are practising on these bees."

Well, you laughed to yourself, "Silly old Bear!" but you didn't say it aloud because you were so fond of him, and you went home for your umbrella.

"Oh, there you are!" called down Winnie-the-Pooh, as soon as you got back to the tree. "I was beginning to get anxious. I have discovered that the bees are now definitely Suspicious."

"Shall I put my umbrella up?" you said.

"Yes, but wait a moment. We must be practical. The

important bee to deceive is the Queen Bee. Can you see which is the Queen Bee from down there?"

"No."

"A pity. Well, now, if you walk up and down with your umbrella, saying, 'Tut-tut, it looks like rain,' I shall do what I can by singing a little Cloud Song, such as a cloud might sing . . . . Go!"

So, while you walked up and down and wondered if it would rain, Winnie-the-Pooh sang this song:

How sweet to be a Cloud
Floating in the Blue!
Every little cloud
Always *sings aloud.*

"How sweet to be a Cloud
Floating in the Blue!"
It makes him very proud
To be a little cloud.

The bees were still buzzing as suspiciously as ever. Some of them, indeed, left their nests and flew all round the cloud as it began the second verse of this song, and one bee sat down on the nose of the cloud for a moment, and then got up again.

"Christopher — *ow!* — Robin," called out the cloud.

"Yes?"

"I have just been thinking, and I have come to a very important decision. *These are the wrong sort of bees.*"

"Are they?"

"Quite the wrong sort. So I should think they would make the wrong sort of honey, shouldn't you?"

"Would they?"

"Yes. So I think I shall come down."

"How?" asked you.

Winnie-the-Pooh hadn't thought about this. If he let go of the string, he would fall – *bump* – and he didn't like the idea of that. So he thought for a long time, and then he said:

"Christopher Robin, you must shoot the balloon with your gun. Have you got your gun?"

"Of course I have," you said. "But if I do that, it will spoil the balloon," you said.

"But if you *don't*," said Pooh, "I shall have to let go, and that would spoil *me*."

When he put it like this, you saw how it was, and you aimed very carefully at the balloon, and fired.

"*Ow!*" said Pooh.

"Did I miss?" you asked.

"You didn't exactly *miss*," said Pooh, "but you missed the *balloon*."

"I'm so sorry," you said, and you fired again, and this time you hit the balloon, and the air came slowly out, and Winnie-the-Pooh floated down to the ground.

But his arms were so stiff from holding on to the string of the balloon all that time that they stayed up straight in the air for more than a week, and whenever a fly came and settled on his nose he had to blow it off. And I think — but I am not sure — that *that* is why he was always called Pooh.

• • • • •

"Is that the end of the story?" asked Christopher Robin.

"That's the end of that one. There are others."

"About Pooh and Me?"

"And Piglet and Rabbit and all of you. Don't you remember?"

"I do remember, and then when I try to remember, I forget."

"That day when Pooh and Piglet tried to catch the Heffalump —"

"They didn't catch it, did they?"

"No."

"Pooh couldn't, because he hasn't any brain. Did *I* catch it?"

"Well, that comes into the story."

Christopher Robin nodded.

"I do remember," he said, "only Pooh doesn't very well, so that's why he likes having it told to him again. Because then it's a real story and not just a remembering."

"That's just how *I* feel," I said.

Christopher Robin gave a deep sigh, picked his Bear up by the leg, and walked off to the door, trailing Pooh behind him. At the door he turned and said, "Coming to see me have my bath?"

"I might," I said.

"I didn't hurt him when I shot him, did I?"

"Not a bit."

He nodded and went out, and in a moment I heard Winnie-the-Pooh — *bump, bump, bump* — going up the stairs behind him.

IN WHICH POOH GOES VISITING AND GETS INTO A TIGHT PLACE

Edward Bear, known to his friends as Winnie-the-Pooh, or Pooh for short, was walking through the forest one day, humming proudly to himself. He had made up a little hum that very morning, as he was doing his Stoutness Exercises in front of the glass:

Tra-la-la, tra-la-la, as he stretched up as high as he could go, and then *Tra-la-la, tra-la — oh, help! — la*, as he tried to reach his toes. After breakfast he had said it over and over to himself until he had learnt it off by heart, and now he was humming it right through, properly. It went like this:

Tra-la-la, tra-la-la,
Tra-la-la, tra-la-la,
Rum-tum-tiddle-um-tum.
Tiddle-iddle, tiddle-iddle,
Tiddle-iddle, tiddle-iddle,
Rum-tum-tum-tiddle-um.

Well, he was humming this hum to himself, and walking gaily along, wondering what everybody else was doing, and what it felt like, being somebody else, when suddenly he came to a sandy bank, and in the bank was a large hole.

"Aha!" said Pooh. (*Rum-tum-tiddle-um-tum.*) "If I know anything about anything, that hole means Rabbit," he said, "and Rabbit means Company," he said, "and Company means Food and Listening-to-Me-Humming and such like. *Rum-tum-tum-tiddle-um.*"

So he bent down, put his head into the hole, and called out:

"Is anybody at home?"

There was a sudden scuffling noise from inside the hole, and then silence.

"What I said was, 'Is anybody at home?'" called out Pooh very loudly.

"No!" said a voice; and then added, "You needn't shout so loud. I heard you quite well the first time."

"Bother!" said Pooh. "Isn't there anybody here at all?"

"Nobody."

Winnie-the-Pooh took his head out of the hole, and thought for a little, and he thought to himself, "There must be somebody there, because somebody must have *said* 'Nobody.'" So he put his head back in the hole, and said:

"Hallo, Rabbit, isn't that you?"

"No," said Rabbit, in a different sort of voice this time.

"But isn't that Rabbit's voice?"

"I don't *think* so," said Rabbit. "It isn't *meant* to be."

"Oh!" said Pooh.

He took his head out of the hole, and had another think, and then he put it back, and said:

"Well, could you very kindly tell me where Rabbit is?"

"He has gone to see his friend Pooh Bear, who is a great friend of his."

"But this *is* Me!" said Bear, very much surprised.

"What sort of Me!"

"Pooh Bear."

"Are you sure?" said Rabbit, still more surprised.

"Quite, quite sure," said Pooh.

"Oh, well, then, come in."

So Pooh pushed and pushed his way through the hole, and at last he got in.

"You were quite right," said Rabbit, looking at him all over. "It *is* you. Glad to see you."

"Who did you think it was?"

"Well, I wasn't sure. You know how it is in the Forest. One can't have *anybody* coming into one's house. One has to be *careful*. What about a mouthful of something?"

Pooh always liked a little something at eleven o'clock in the morning, and he was very glad to see Rabbit getting out the plates and mugs; and when Rabbit said, "Honey or condensed milk with your bread?" he was so excited that he said, "Both," and then, so as not to seem greedy, he added, "But don't bother about the bread, please." And for a long time after that he said nothing . . . until at last, humming to himself in a rather sticky voice, he got up, shook Rabbit lovingly by the paw, and said that he must be going on.

"Must you?" said Rabbit politely.

"Well," said Pooh, "I could stay a little longer if it — if you —" and he tried very hard to look in the direction of the larder.

"As a matter of fact," said Rabbit, "I was going out myself directly."

"Oh well, then, I'll be going on. Good-bye."

"Well, good-bye, if you're sure you won't have any more."

"Is there any more?" said Pooh quickly.

Rabbit took the covers off the dishes, and said, "No, there wasn't."

"I thought not," said Pooh, nodding to himself. "Well, good-bye. I must be going on."

So he started to climb out of the hole. He pulled with his front paws, and pushed with his back paws, and in a little while his nose was out in the open again . . . and then his ears . . . and then his front paws . . . and then his shoulders . . . and then —

"Oh, help!" said Pooh.

"I'd better go back."

"Oh, bother!" said Pooh. "I shall have to go on."

"I can't do either!" said Pooh. "Oh, help *and* bother!"

Now, by this time Rabbit wanted to go for a walk too, and finding the front door full, he went out by the back door, and came round to Pooh, and looked at him.

"Hallo, are you stuck?" he asked.

"N-no," said Pooh carelessly.

"Just resting and thinking and humming to myself."

"Here, give us a paw."

Pooh Bear stretched out a paw, and Rabbit pulled and pulled and pulled. . . .

"*Ow!*" cried Pooh. "You're hurting!"

"The fact is," said Rabbit, "You're stuck."

"It all comes," said Pooh crossly, "of not having front doors big enough."

"It all comes," said Rabbit sternly, "of eating too much. I thought at the time," said Rabbit, "only I didn't like to say anything," said Rabbit, "that one of us was eating too much," said Rabbit, "and I knew it wasn't *me*," he said. "Well, well, I shall go and fetch Christopher Robin."

Christopher Robin lived at the other end of the Forest, and when he came back with Rabbit, and saw the front half of Pooh, he said, "Silly old Bear," in such a loving voice that everybody felt quite hopeful again.

"I was just beginning to think," said Bear, sniffing slightly, "that Rabbit might never be able to use his front door again. And I should *hate* that," he said.

"So should I," said Rabbit.

"Use his front door again?" said Christopher Robin. "Of course he'll use his front door again."

"Good," said Rabbit.

"If we can't pull you out, Pooh, we might push you back."

Rabbit scratched his whiskers thoughtfully, and pointed out that, when once Pooh was pushed back, he was back, and of course nobody was more glad to see Pooh than *he* was, still there it was, some lived in trees and some lived underground, and —

"You mean I'd *never* get out?" said Pooh.

"I mean," said Rabbit, "that having got *so* far, it seems a pity to waste it."

Christopher Robin nodded.

"Then there's only one thing to be done," he said. "We shall have to wait for you to get thin again."

"How long does getting thin take?" asked Pooh anxiously.

"About a week, I should think."

"But I can't stay here for a *week*!"

"You can *stay* here all right, silly old Bear. It's getting you out which is so difficult."

"We'll read to you," said Rabbit cheerfully.

"And I hope it won't snow," he added. "And I say, old fellow, you're taking up a good deal of room in my house — *do* you mind if I use your back legs as a towel-horse? Because, I mean, there they are — doing nothing — and it would be very convenient just to hang the towels on them."

"A week!" said Pooh gloomily. "*What about meals?*"

"I'm afraid no meals," said Christopher Robin, because of getting thin quicker. But we *will* read to you."

Bear began to sigh, and then found he couldn't because he was so tightly stuck; and a tear rolled down his eye, as he said:

"Then would you read a Sustaining Book, such as would help and comfort a Wedged Bear in Great Tightness?"

So for a week Christopher Robin read that sort of book at the North end of Pooh,

and Rabbit hung his washing on the South end . . .

and in between Bear felt himself getting slenderer and slenderer. And at the end of the week Christopher Robin said, "*Now!*"

So he took hold of Pooh's front paws and Rabbit took hold of Christopher Robin, and all Rabbit's friends and relations took hold of Rabbit and they all pulled together. . . .

And for a long time Pooh only said "*Ow!*" . . .

And "*Oh!*" . . .

And then, all of a sudden, he said "*Pop!*" just as if a cork were coming out of a bottle.

And Christopher Robin and Rabbit and all Rabbit's friends and relations went head-over-heels backwards . . . and on the top of them came Winnie-the-Pooh — free!

So, with a nod of thanks to his friends, he went on with his walk through the forest, humming proudly to himself. But Christopher Robin looked after him lovingly, and said to himself, "Silly old Bear!"

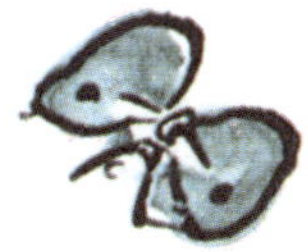

Hoppity

Christopher Robin goes
Hoppity, hoppity,

Hoppity, hoppity, hop,
Whenever I tell him
Politely to stop it, he
Says he can't possibly stop.

If he stopped hopping, he couldn't go anywhere,
Poor little Christopher
Couldn't go anywhere . . .
That's why he always goes
Hoppity, hoppity,
Hoppity,
Hoppity,
Hop.

Furry Bear

If I were a bear,
And a big bear too,
I shouldn't much care
If it froze or snew;
I shouldn't much mind
If it snowed or friz —
I'd be all fur-lined
With a coat like his!

For I'd have fur boots and a brown fur wrap,
And brown fur knickers and a big fur cap.
I'd have a fur muffle-ruff to cover my jaws,
And brown fur mittens on my big brown paws.
With a big brown furry-down up to my head,
I'd sleep all the winter in a big fur bed.

Buckingham Palace

They're changing guard at Buckingham Palace —
Christopher Robin went down with Alice.
Alice is marrying one of the guard.
"A soldier's life is terrible hard,"
Says Alice.

They're changing guard at Buckingham Palace —
Christopher Robin went down with Alice.
We saw a guard in a sentry-box.
"One of the sergeants looks after their socks,"
Says Alice.

They're changing guard at Buckingham Palace —
Christopher Robin went down with Alice.
We looked for the King, but he never came.
"Well, God take care of him, all the same,"
Says Alice.

They're changing guard at Buckingham Palace —
Christopher Robin went down with Alice.
They've great big parties inside the grounds.
"I wouldn't be King for a hundred pounds,"
Says Alice.

They're changing guard at Buckingham Palace —
Christopher Robin went down with Alice.
A face looked out, but it wasn't the King's.
"He's much too busy a-signing things,"
Says Alice.

They're changing guard at Buckingham Palace —
Christopher Robin went down with Alice.
"Do you think the King knows all about me?"
"Sure to, dear, but it's time for tea,"
Says Alice.

IN WHICH EEYORE LOSES A TAIL AND POOH FINDS ONE

The Old Grey Donkey, Eeyore, stood by himself in a thistly corner of the Forest, his front feet well apart, his head on one side, and thought about things. Sometimes he

thought sadly to himself, "Why?" and sometimes he thought, "Wherefore?" and sometimes he thought, "Inasmuch as

which?" — and sometimes he didn't quite know what he *was* thinking about. So when Winnie-the-Pooh came stumping along, Eeyore was very glad to be able to stop thinking for a little, in order to say "How do you do?" in a gloomy manner to him.

"And how are you?" said Winnie-the-Pooh.

Eeyore shook his head from side to side.

"Not very how," he said. "I don't seem to have felt at all how for a long time."

"Dear, dear," said Pooh, "I'm sorry about that. Let's have a look at you."

So Eeyore stood there, gazing sadly at the ground, and Winnie-the-Pooh walked all round him once.

"Why, what's happened to your tail?" he said in surprise.

"What *has* happened to it?" said Eeyore.

"It isn't there!"

"Are you sure?"

"Well, either a tail *is* there or it isn't there. You can't make a mistake about it, and yours *isn't* there!"

"Then what is?"

"Nothing."

"Let's have a look," said Eeyore, and he turned slowly round to the place where his tail had been a little while ago, and then, finding that he couldn't catch it up, he turned round the other way, until he came back to where he was at first, and then he put his head down and looked between his front legs, and at last he said, with a long, sad sigh, "I believe you're right."

"Of course I'm right," said Pooh.

"That Accounts for a Good Deal," said Eeyore gloomily.

"It Explains Everything. No Wonder."

"You must have left it somewhere," said Winnie-the-Pooh.

"Somebody must have taken it," said Eeyore. "How Like Them," he added, after a long silence.

Pooh felt that he ought to say something helpful about it, but didn't quite know what. So he decided to do something helpful instead.

"Eeyore," he said solemnly, "I, Winnie-the-Pooh, will find your tail for you."

"Thank you, Pooh," answered Eeyore. "You're a real friend," said he. "Not Like Some," he said.

So Winnie-the-Pooh went off to find Eeyore's tail.

It was a fine spring morning in the Forest as he started out. Little soft clouds played happily in a blue sky, skipping from time to time in front of the sun as if they had come to put it out, and then sliding away suddenly so that the next might have his turn. Through them and between them the sun shone bravely; and a copse which had worn its firs all the year round seemed old and dowdy now beside the new green lace which the beeches had put on so prettily. Through copse and spinney marched Bear; down open slopes of gorse and heather, over rocky beds of streams, up steep banks of sandstone into the heather again; and so at last, tired and hungry, to the Hundred Acre Wood. For it was in the Hundred Acre Wood that Owl lived.

"And if anyone knows anything about anything," said Bear to himself, "it's Owl who knows something about something," he said, "or my name's not Winnie-the-Pooh," he said, "Which it is," he added, "So there you are."

Owl lived at The Chestnuts, an old-world residence of great charm, which was grander than anybody else's, or

seemed so to Bear, because it had both a knocker *and* a bell-pull. Underneath the knocker there was a notice which said.

PLES RING IF AN RNSER IS REQIRD.

Underneath the bell-pull there was a notice which said:

PLEZ CNOKE IF AN RNSR IS NOT REQID.

These notices had been written by Christopher Robin, who was the only one in the forest who could spell; for Owl, wise though he was in many ways, able to read and write and spell his own name WOL, yet somehow went all to pieces over delicate words like MEASLES and BUTTEREDTOAST.

Winnie-the-Pooh read the two notices very carefully, first from left to right, and afterwards, in case he had missed some of it, from right to left. Then, to make quite sure, he knocked and pulled the knocker, and he pulled and knocked the bell-rope, and he called out in a very loud voice, "Owl! I require an answer! It's Bear speaking." And the door opened, and Owl looked out.

"Hallo, Pooh," he said. "How's things?"

"Terrible and Sad," said Pooh, "because Eeyore, who is a friend of mine, has lost his tail. And he's Moping about it. So could you very kindly tell me how to find it for him?"

"Well," said Owl, "the customary procedure in such cases is as follows."

"What does Crustimoney Proseedcake mean?" said Pooh. "For I am a Bear of Very Little Brain, and long words Bother me."

"It means the Thing to Do."

PLES RING
IF AN RNSER
IS REQIRD
PLEZ CNOKE
IF AN RNSR
IS NOT REQID

"As long as it means that, I don't mind," said Pooh humbly.

"The thing to do is as follows. First, Issue a Reward. Then —"

"Just a moment," said Pooh, holding up his paw. "*What* do we do to this — what were you saying? You sneezed just as you were going to tell me."

"I *didn't* sneeze."

"Yes, you did, Owl."

"Excuse me, Pooh, I didn't. You can't sneeze without knowing it."

"Well, you can't know it without something having been sneezed."

"What I *said* was, 'First *Issue* a Reward'."

"You're doing it again," said Pooh sadly.

"A Reward!" said Owl very loudly. "We write a notice to

say that we will give a large something to anybody who finds Eeyore's tail."

"I see, I see," said Pooh, nodding his head. "Talking about large somethings," he went on dreamily, "I generally have a small something about now — about this time in the morning," and he looked wistfully at the cupboard in the corner of Owl's parlour; "just a mouthful of condensed milk or what-not, with perhaps a lick of honey —"

"Well, then," said Owl, "we write out this notice, and we put it up all over the Forest."

"A lick of honey," murmured Bear to himself, "or — or not, as the case may be." And he gave a deep sigh, and tried very hard to listen to what Owl was saying.

But Owl went on and on, using longer and longer words, until at last he came back to where he started, and he explained that the person to write out this notice was Christopher Robin.

"It was he who wrote the ones on my front door for me. Did you see them, Pooh?"

For some time now Pooh had been saying "Yes" and "No" in turn, with his eyes shut, to all that Owl was saying, and having said, "Yes, yes," last time, he said, "No, not at all," now, without really knowing what Owl was talking about.

"Didn't you see them?" said Owl, a little surprised. "Come and look at them now."

So they went outside. And Pooh looked at the knocker and the notice below it, and he looked at the bell-rope and the notice below it, and the more he looked at the bell-rope, the more he felt that he had seen something like it, somewhere else, sometime before.

"Handsome bell-rope, isn't it?" said Owl.

Pooh nodded.

"It reminds me of something," he said, "but I can't think what. Where did you get it?"

"I just came across it in the Forest. It was hanging over a bush, and I thought at first somebody lived there, so I rang it, and nothing happened, and then I rang it again very loudly, and it came off in my hand, and as nobody seemed to want it, I took it home, and —"

"Owl," said Pooh solemnly, "you made a mistake. Somebody did want it."

"Who?"

"Eeyore. My dear friend Eeyore. He was — he was fond of it."

"Fond of it?"

"Attached to it," said Winnie-the-Pooh sadly.

. . . . . .

So with those words he unhooked it, and carried it back to Eeyore; and when Christopher Robin had nailed it on in its

right place again, Eeyore frisked about the forest, waving his tail so happily that Winnie-the-Pooh came over all funny, and had to hurry home for a little snack of something to sustain him. And, wiping his mouth half an hour afterwards, he sang to himself proudly:

Who found the Tail?
"I," said Pooh,
"At a quarter to two
(Only it was quarter to eleven really),
I *found the Tail!"*

IN WHICH TIGGER COMES TO THE FOREST AND HAS BREAKFAST

Winnie-the-Pooh woke up suddenly in the middle of the night and listened. Then he got out of bed, and lit his candle, and stumped across the room to see if anybody was trying to get into his honey-cupboard, and they weren't, so he stumped back again, blew out his candle, and got into bed. Then he heard the noise again.

"Is that you, Piglet?" he said.

But it wasn't.

"Come in, Christopher Robin," he said.

But Christopher Robin didn't.

"Tell me about it to-morrow, Eeyore," said Pooh sleepily.

But the noise went on.

"*Worraworraworraworraworra,*" said Whatever-it-was, and Pooh found that he wasn't asleep after all.

"What can it be?" he thought. "There are lots of noises in the Forest, but this is a different one. It isn't a growl, and it

isn't a purr, and it isn't a bark, and it isn't the noise-you-make-before-beginning-a-piece-of-poetry, but it's a noise of some kind, made by a strange animal! And he's making it outside my door. So I shall get up and ask him not to do it."

He got out of bed and opened his front door.

"Hallo!" said Pooh, in case there was anything outside.

"Hallo!" said Whatever-it-was.

"Oh!" said Pooh. "Hallo!"

"Hallo!"

"Oh, *there* you are!" said Pooh. "Hallo!"

"Hallo!" said the Strange Animal, wondering how long this was going on.

Pooh was just going to say "Hallo!" for the fourth time when he thought that he wouldn't, so he said, "Who is it?" instead.

"Me," said a voice.

"Oh!" said Pooh. "Well, come here,"

So Whatever-it-was came here, and in the light of the candle he and Pooh looked at each other.

"I'm Pooh," said Pooh.

"I'm Tigger," said Tigger.

"Oh!" said Pooh, for he had never seen an animal like this before. "Does Christopher Robin know about you?"

"Of course he does," said Tigger.

"Well," said Pooh, "it's the middle of the night, which is a good time for going to sleep. And to-morrow morning we'll have some honey for breakfast. Do Tiggers like honey?"

"They like everything," said Tigger cheerfully.

"Then if they like going to sleep on the floor, I'll go back to bed," said Pooh, "and we'll do things in the morning. Good night." And he got back into bed and went fast asleep.

When he awoke in the morning, the first thing he saw was Tigger, sitting in front of the glass and looking at himself.

"Hallo!" said Pooh.

"Hallo!" said Tigger. "I've found somebody just like me. I thought I was the only one of them."

Pooh got out of bed, and began to explain what a looking-glass was, but just as he was getting to the interesting part,

Tigger said:

"Excuse me a moment, but there's something climbing up your table," and with one loud *Worraworraworraworraworra* he jumped at the end of the tablecloth, pulled it to the ground, wrapped himself up in it three times, rolled to the other end of the room, and, after a terrible struggle, got his head into the daylight again, and said cheerfully: "Have I won?"

"That's my tablecloth," said Pooh, as he began to unwind Tigger.

"I wondered what it was," said Tigger.

"It goes on the table and you put things on it."

"Then why did it try to bite me when I wasn't looking?"

"I don't *think* it did," said Pooh.

"It tried," said Tigger, "but I was too quick for it."

Pooh put the cloth back on the table, and he put a large honey-pot on the cloth, and they sat down to breakfast. And as soon as they sat down, Tigger took a large mouthful of honey . . . and he looked up at the ceiling with his head on

one side, and made exploring noises with his tongue, and considering noises, and what-have-we-got-*here* noises . . . and then he said in a very decided voice:

"Tiggers don't like honey."

"Oh!" said Pooh, and tried to make it sound Sad and Regretful. "I thought they liked everything."

"Everything except honey," said Tigger.

Pooh felt rather pleased about this, and said that, as soon as he had finished his own breakfast, he would take Tigger round to Piglet's house, and Tigger could try some of Piglet's haycorns.

"Thank you, Pooh," said Tigger, "because haycorns is really what Tiggers like best."

So after breakfast they went round to see Piglet, and Pooh explained as they went that Piglet was a Very Small Animal who didn't like bouncing, and asked Tigger not be too Bouncy just at first. And Tigger, who had been hiding behind trees and jumping out on Pooh's shadow when it wasn't looking, said that Tiggers were only bouncy before breakfast, and that as soon as they had had a few haycorns they became Quiet and Refined. So by-and-by they knocked at the door of Piglet's house.

"Hallo, Pooh," said Piglet.

"Hallo, Piglet. This is Tigger.

"Oh, is it?" said Piglet, and he edged round to the other side of the table. "I thought Tiggers were smaller than that."

"Not the big ones," said Tigger.

"They like haycorns," said Pooh, "so that's what we've come for, because poor Tigger hasn't had any breakfast yet."

Piglet pushed the bowl of haycorns towards Tigger, and said, "Help yourself," and then he got close up to Pooh and

felt much braver, and said, "So you're Tigger? Well, well!" in a careless sort of voice. But Tigger said nothing because his mouth was full of haycorns. . . .

After a long munching noise he said:

"Ee-ers o i a-ors."

And when Pooh and Piglet said "What?" he said "Skoos ee," and went outside for a moment.

When he came back he said firmly:

"Tiggers don't like haycorns."

"But you said they liked everything except honey," said Pooh.

"Everything except honey *and* haycorns," explained Tigger.

When he heard this, Pooh said, "Oh, I see!" and Piglet, who was rather glad that Tiggers didn't like haycorns, said, "What about thistles?"

"Thistles," said Tigger, "is what Tiggers like best."

"Then let's go along and see Eeyore," said Piglet.

So the three of them went; and after they had walked and walked and walked, they came to the part of the Forest where Eeyore was.

"Hallo, Eeyore!" said Pooh. "This is Tigger."

"What is?" said Eeyore.

"This," explained Pooh and Piglet together, and Tigger smiled his happiest smile and said nothing.

Eeyore walked all round Tigger one way, and then turned and walked all round him the other way.

"What did you say it was?" he asked.

"Tigger."

"Ah!" said Eeyore.

"He's just come," explained Piglet.

"Ah!" said Eeyore again.

He thought for a long time and then said:

"When is he going?"

Pooh explained to Eeyore that Tigger was a great friend of Christopher Robin's, who had come to stay in the Forest, and Piglet explained to Tigger that he mustn't mind what Eeyore said because he was *always* gloomy; and Eeyore explained to

Piglet that, on the contrary, he was feeling particularly cheerful this morning; and Tigger explained to anybody who was listening that he hadn't had any breakfast yet.

"I knew there was something," said Pooh. "Tiggers always eat thistles, so that was why we came to see you, Eeyore."Don't mention it, Pooh."

"Oh, Eeyore, I didn't mean that I didn't *want* to see you —"

"Quite — quite. But your new stripy friend — naturally, he wants his breakfast. What did you say his name was?"

"Tigger."

"Then come this way, Tigger."

Eeyore led the way to the most thistly-looking patch of thistles that ever was, and waved a hoof at it.

"A little patch I was keeping for my birthday," he said; "but, after all, what *are* birthdays? Here to-day and gone to-morrow. Help yourself, Tigger."

Tigger thanked him and looked a little anxiously at Pooh.

"Are these really thistles?" he whispered.

"Yes," said Pooh.

"What Tiggers like best?"

"That's right," said Pooh.

"I see," said Tigger.

So he took a large mouthful, and he gave a large crunch.

"*Ow!*" said Tigger.

He sat down and put his paw in his mouth.

"What's the matter?" asked Pooh.

"*Hot!* mumbled Tigger.

"Your friend," said Eeyore, "appears to have bitten on a bee."

Pooh's friend stopped shaking his head to get the prickles out, and explained that Tiggers didn't like thistles.

"Then why bend a perfectly good one?" asked Eeyore.

"But you said," began Pooh, " — you *said* that Tiggers liked everything except honey and haycorns."

"*And* thistles," said Tigger, who was now running round in circles with his tongue hanging out.

Pooh looked at him sadly.

"What are we going to do?" he asked Piglet.

Piglet knew the answer to that, and he said at once that they must go and see Christopher Robin.

"You'll find him with Kanga," said Eeyore. He came close to Pooh, and said in a loud whisper:

"*Could* you ask your friend to do his exercises somewhere else? I shall be having lunch directly, and don't want it bounced on just before I begin. A trifling matter, and fussy of me, but we all have our little ways."

Pooh nodded solemnly and called to Tigger.

"Come along and we'll go and see Kanga. She's sure to have lots of breakfast for you."

Tigger finished his last circle and came up to Pooh and Piglet.

"Hot!" he explained with a large and friendly smile. "Come on!" and he rushed off.

Pooh and Piglet walked slowly after him. And as they walked Piglet said nothing, because he couldn't think of

anything, and Pooh said nothing, because he was thinking of a poem. And when he had thought of it he began:

What shall we do about poor little Tigger?
If he never eats nothing he'll never get bigger.
He doesn't like honey and haycorns and thistles
Because of the taste and because of the bristles.
And all the good things which an animal likes
Have the wrong sort of swallow or too many spikes.

"He's quite big enough anyhow," said Piglet.

"He isn't *really* very big."

"Well, he *seems* so."

Pooh was thoughtful when he heard this, and then he murmured to himself:

But whatever his weight in pounds, shillings, and
ounces,
He always seems bigger because of his bounces.

"And that's the whole poem," he said. "Do you like it, Piglet?"

"All except the shillings," said Piglet. "I don't think they ought to be there."

"They wanted to come in after the pounds," explained Pooh, 'so I let them. It is the best way to write poetry, letting things come."

"Oh, I didn't know," said Piglet.

Tigger had been bouncing in front of them all this time, turning round every now and then to ask, "Is this the way?" — and now at last they came in sight of Kanga's house, and there was Christopher Robin. Tigger rushed up to him.

"Oh, there you are, Tigger!" said Christopher Robin. "I knew you'd be somewhere."

"I've been finding things in the Forest," said Tigger

importantly. "I've found a pooh and a piglet and an eeyore, but I can't find any breakfast."

Pooh and Piglet came up and hugged Christopher Robin, and explained what had been happening.

"Don't *you* know what Tiggers like?" asked Pooh.

"I expect if I thought very hard I should," said Christopher Robin, "but I *thought* Tigger knew."

"I do," said Tigger. "Everything there is in the world except honey and haycorns and — what were those hot things called?"

"Thistles."

"Yes, and those."

"Oh, well then, Kanga can give you some breakfast."

So they went into Kanga's house, and when Roo had said, "Hallo, Pooh," and "Hallo, Piglet" once, and "Hallo, Tigger" twice, because he had never said it before and it sounded funny, they told Kanga what they wanted, and Kanga said very kindly, "Well, look in my cupboard, Tigger dear, and see what you'd like." Because she knew at once that, however big Tigger seemed to be, he wanted as much kindness as Roo.

"Shall I look, too?" said Pooh, who was beginning to feel a little eleven o'clockish. And he found a small tin of condensed milk, and something seemed to tell him that Tiggers didn't like this, so he took it into a corner by itself, and went with it to see that nobody interrupted it.

But the more Tigger put his nose into this and his paw into that, the more things he found which Tiggers didn't like. And when he

had found everything in the cupboard, and couldn't eat any of it, he said to Kanga, "What happens now?"

But Kanga and Christopher Robin and Piglet were all standing round Roo, watching him have his Extract of Malt. And Roo was saying, "Must I?" and Kanga was saying, "Now, Roo dear, you remember what you promised."

"What is it?" whispered Tigger to Piglet.

"His Strengthening Medicine," said Piglet. "He hates it."

So Tigger came closer, and he leant over the back of Roo's chair, and suddenly he put out his tongue, and took one large golollop, and, with a sudden jump of surprise, Kanga said, "Oh!" and then clutched at the spoon again just as it was disappearing, and pulled it safely back out of Tigger's mouth. But the Extract of Malt had gone.

"Tigger *dear*!" said Kanga.

"He's taken my medicine, he's taken my medicine, he's taken my medicine!" sang Roo happily, thinking it was a tremendous joke.

Then Tigger looked up at the ceiling, and closed his eyes, and his tongue went round and round his chops, in case he had

left any outside, and a peaceful smile came over his face as he said. "So *that's* what Tiggers like!"

. . . . . .

Which explains why he always lived at Kanga's house afterwards, and had Extract of Malt for breakfast, dinner, and tea. And sometimes, when Kanga thought he wanted strengthening, he had a spoonful or two of Roosbreakfast after meals as medicine.

"But *I* think," said Piglet to Pooh, "that he's been strengthened quite enough."

Us Two

Wherever I am, there's always Pooh,
There's always Pooh, and Me.
Whatever I do, he wants to do,
Where are you going to-day?" says Pooh:
Well, that's very odd 'cos I was too.
Let's go together," says Pooh, says he.
Let's go together," says Pooh.

What's twice eleven?" I said to Pooh,
"Twice what?" said Pooh to Me.
"I think it ought to be twenty-two.
Just what I think myself," said Pooh.
It wasn't an easy sum to do,
But that's what it is," said Pooh, said he.
That's what it is," said Pooh.

"Let's look for dragons," I said to Pooh.
"Yes, let's," said Pooh to Me
We crossed the river and found a few —
"Yes, those are dragons all right," said Pooh.
"As soon as I saw their beaks I knew.
That's what they are," said Pooh, said he.
"That's what they are," said Pooh.

"Let's frighten the dragons," I said to Pooh.
"That's right," said Pooh to Me.
"I'm *not afraid," I said to Pooh,*
And I held his paw and I shouted "Shoo!
Silly old dragons!" — and off they flew.
"I wasn't afraid," said Pooh, said he,
"I'm never *afraid with you."*

So wherever I am, there's always Pooh,
There's always Pooh and Me.
"What would I do?" I said to Pooh,
"If it wasn't for you," and Pooh said: "True,
It isn't much fun for One, but Two
Can stick together," says Pooh, says he.
"That's how it is," says Pooh.

A Thought

If I were John and John were Me,
Then he'd be six and I'd be three.
If John were Me and I were John,
I shouldn't have these trousers on.

Lines and Squares

Whenever I walk in a London street,
I'm ever so careful to watch my feet;
And I keep in the squares,
And the masses of bears,
Who wait at the corners all ready to eat
The sillies who tread on the lines of the street,
Go back to their lairs,
And I say to them, "Bears,
Just look how I'm walking in all the squares!"

And the little bears growl to each other, "He's mine,
As soon as he's silly and steps on a line."
And some of the bigger bears try to pretend
That they came round the corner to look for a friend;
And they try to pretend that nobody cares
Whether you walk on the lines or squares.
But only the sillies believe their talk;
It's ever so portant how you walk.
And it's ever so jolly to call out, "Bears,
Just watch me walking in all the squares!"

IN WHICH PIGLET MEETS A HEFFALUMP

One day, when Christopher Robin and Winnie-the-Pooh and Piglet were all talking together, Christopher Robin finished the mouthful he was eating and said carelessly: "I saw a Heffalump to-day, Piglet."

"What was it doing?" asked Piglet.

"Just lumping along," said Christopher Robin. "I don't think it saw *me*."

"I saw one once," said Piglet. "I think I did," he said. "Only perhaps it wasn't."

"So did I," said Pooh, wondering what a Heffalump was like.

"You don't often see them," said Christopher Robin carelessly.

"Not now," said Piglet.

"Not at this time of year," said Pooh.

Then they all talked about something else, until it was time for Pooh and Piglet to go home together. At first as they stumped along the path which edged the Hundred Acre Wood, they didn't say much to each other; but when they came to the stream, and had helped each other across the

stepping stones, and were able to walk side by side again over the heather, they began to talk in a friendly way about this and that, and Piglet said, "If you see what I mean, Pooh," and Pooh said, "It's just what I think myself, Piglet," and Piglet said, "But, on the other hand, Pooh, we must remember," and Pooh said, "Quite true, Piglet, although I had forgotten it for the moment." And then, just as they came to the Six Pine Trees, Pooh looked round to see that nobody else was listening, and said in a very solemn voice;

"Piglet, I have decided something."

"What have you decided, Pooh?"

"I have decided to catch a Heffalump."

Pooh nodded his head several times as he said this, and waited for Piglet to say "How?" or "Pooh, you couldn't!" or something helpful of that sort, but Piglet said nothing. The fact was Piglet was wishing that *he* had thought about it first.

"I shall do it," said Pooh, after waiting a little longer, "by means of a trap. And it must be a Cunning Trap, so you will have to help me, Piglet."

"Pooh," said Piglet, feeling quite happy again now, "I

will." And then he said, "How shall we do it?" and Pooh said, "That's just it. How?" And then they sat down together to think it out.

Pooh's first idea was that they should dig a Very Deep Pit, and then the Heffalump would come along and fall into the Pit, and —

"Why?" said Piglet.

"Why what?" said Pooh.

"Why would he fall in?"

Pooh rubbed his nose with his paw, and said that the Heffalump might be walking along, humming a little song, and looking up at the sky, wondering if it would rain, and so he wouldn't see the Very Deep Pit until he was half-way down, when it would be too late.

Piglet said that this was a very good Trap, but supposing it were raining already?

Pooh rubbed his nose again, and said that he hadn't thought of that. And then he brightened up, and said that, if it were raining already, the Heffalump would be looking at the sky wondering if it would *clear up*, and so he wouldn't see the Very Deep pit until he was half-way down. . . . When it would be too late.

Piglet said that, now that this point had been explained, he thought it was a Cunning Trap.

Pooh was very proud when he heard this, and he felt that the Heffalump was as good as caught already, but there was just one other thing which had to be thought about, and it was this. *Where should they dig the Very Deep Pit?*

Piglet said that the best place would be somewhere a Heffalump was, just before he fell into it, only about a foot further on.

"But then he would see us digging it," said Pooh.

"Not if he was looking at the sky."

"He would Suspect," said Pooh, "if he happened to look down." He thought for a long time and then added sadly, "It isn't as easy as I thought. I suppose that's why Heffalumps hardly *ever* get caught."

"That must be it," said Piglet.

They sighed and got up; and when they had taken a few gorse prickles out of themselves they sat down again; and all the time Pooh was saying to himself, "If only I could *think* of something!" For he felt sure that a Very Clever Brain could catch a Heffalump if only he knew the right way to go about it.

"Suppose," he said to Piglet, "*you* wanted to catch *me*, how would you do it?"

"Well," said Piglet, "I should do it like this. I should make a Trap, and I should put a Jar of Honey in the Trap, and you would smell it, and you would go in after it, and —"

"And I would go in after it," said Pooh excitedly, "only very carefully so as not to hurt myself, and I would get to the Jar of Honey, and I should lick round the edges first of all, pretending that there wasn't any more, you know, and then I should walk away and think about it a little, and then I should come back and start licking in the middle of the jar, and then —"

"Yes, well never mind about that. There you would be, and there I should catch you. Now the first thing to think of is, What do Heffalumps like? I should think acorns, shouldn't you? We'll get a lot of — I say, wake up, Pooh!"

Pooh, who had gone into a happy dream, woke up with a start, and said that Honey was a much more trappy thing than

Haycorns. Piglet didn't think so; and they were just going to argue about it, when Piglet remembered that, if they put acorns in the Trap, *he* would have to find the acorns, but if they put honey, then Pooh would have to give up some of his own honey, so he said, "All right, honey then," just as Pooh remembered it too, and was going to say, "All right, haycorns."

"Honey," said Piglet to himself in a thoughtful way, as if it were now settled. "*I'll* dig the pit, while *you* go and get the honey."

"Very well," said Pooh, and he stumped off.

As soon as he got home, he went to the larder; and he stood on a chair, and took down a very large jar of honey from the top shelf. It had HUNNY written on it, but, just to make sure, he took off the paper cover and looked at it, and it *looked* just like honey. "But you never can tell," said Pooh. "I remember my

uncle saying once that he had seen cheese just this colour." So he put his tongue in, and took a large lick. "Yes," he said, "it is. No doubt about that. And honey, I should say, right down to the bottom of the jar. Unless, of course," he said, "somebody put cheese in at the bottom just for a joke. Perhaps I

had better go a *little* further . . . just in case . . . in case Heffalumps *don't* like cheese . . . same as me. . . . Ah!" And he gave a deep sigh. "I *was* right. It *is* honey, right the way down."

Having made certain of this, he took the jar back to Piglet, and Piglet looked up from the bottom of his Very Deep Pit, and said, "Got it?" and Pooh said, "Yes, but it isn't quite a full jar," and he threw it down to Piglet, and Piglet said, "No, it isn't! Is that all you've got left?" and Pooh said, "Yes." Because it was. So Piglet put the jar at the bottom of the Pit, and climbed out, and they went off home together.

"Well, good night, Pooh," said Piglet, when they had got to Pooh's house. "And we meet at six o'clock to-morrow morning by the Pine Trees, and see how many Heffalumps we've got in our Trap."

"Six o'clock, Piglet. And have you got any string?"

"No. why do you want string?"

"To lead them home with."

"Oh! . . . I *think* Heffalumps come if you whistle."

"Some do and some don't. You never can tell with Heffalumps. Well, good night!"

"Good night!"

And off Piglet trotted to his house TRESPASSERS W, while Pooh made his preparations for bed.

Some hours later, just as the night was beginning to steal away, Pooh woke up suddenly with a sinking feeling. He had

had that sinking feeling before, and he knew what it meant. *He was hungry*. So he went to the larder, and he stood on a chair and reached up to the top shelf, and found — nothing.

"That's funny," he thought. "I know I had a jar of honey there. A full jar, full of honey right up to the top, and it had HUNNY written on it, so that I should know it was honey. That's very funny." And then he began to wander up and down, wondering where it was and murmuring a murmur to himself. Like this:

It's very, very funny,
'Cos I know *I had some honey;*
'Cos it had a label on,
Saying HUNNY.

A goloptious full-up pot too,
And I don't know where it's got to,
No, I don't know where it's gone —
Well, it's funny.

He had murmured this to himself three times in a singing sort of way, when suddenly he remembered. He had put it into the Cunning Trap to catch the Heffalump.

"Bother!" said Pooh. "It all comes of trying to be kind to Heffalumps." And he got back into bed.

But he couldn't sleep. The more he tried to sleep, the more he couldn't. He tried Counting Sheep, which is sometimes a good way of getting to sleep, and, as that was no good, he tried counting Heffalumps. And that was worse. Because every Heffalump that he counted was making straight for a pot of Pooh's honey, *and eating it all*. For some minutes he lay there miserably, but when the five hundred and eighty-

seventh Heffalump was licking its jaws, and saying to itself, "Very good honey this, I don't know when I've tasted better," Pooh could bear it no longer. He jumped out of bed, he ran out of the house, and he ran straight to the Six Pine Trees.

The Sun was still in bed, but there was a lightness in the sky over the Hundred Acre Wood which seemed to show that it was waking up and would soon be kicking off the clothes. In the half-light the Pine Trees looked cold and lonely, and the Very Deep Pit seemed deeper than it was, and Pooh's jar of honey at the bottom was something mysterious, a shape and no more. But as he got nearer to it his nose told him that it was indeed honey, and his tongue came out and began to polish up his mouth, ready for it.

"Bother!" said Pooh, as he got his nose inside the jar. "A Heffalump has been eating it!" And then he thought a little and said, "Oh, no, *I* did. I forgot."

Indeed, he had eaten most of it. But there was a little left at the very bottom of the jar, and he pushed his head right in, and began to lick. . . .

By and by Piglet woke up. As soon as he woke he said to himself. "Oh!" Then he said bravely, "Yes," and then, still more bravely, "Quite so." But he didn't feel very brave, for the word which was really jiggeting about in his brain was "Heffalumps."

What was a Heffalump like?

Was it Fierce?

Did it come when you whistled? And *how* did it come?

Was it Fond of Pigs at all?

If it was Fond of Pigs, did it make any difference *what sort of Pig*?

Supposing it was Fierce with Pigs, would it make any difference *if the Pig had a grandfather called TRESPASSERS WILLIAM*?

He didn't know the answer to any of these questions . . . and he was going to see his first Heffalump in about an hour from now!

Of course Pooh would be with him, and it was much more Friendly with two. But suppose Heffalumps were Very Fierce with Pigs *and* Bears? Wouldn't it be better to pretend that he had a headache, and couldn't go up to the Six Pine Trees this

morning? But then suppose that it was a very fine day, and there was no Heffalump in the trap, here he would be, in bed all the morning, simply wasting his time for nothing. What should he do?

And then he had a Clever Idea. He would go up very quietly to the Six Pine Trees now, peep very cautiously into the trap, and see if there *was* a Heffalump there. And if there was, he would go back to bed, and if there wasn't he wouldn't.

So off he went. At first he thought that there wouldn't be a Heffalump in the Trap, and then he thought that there would, and as he got nearer he was *sure* that there would, because he could hear it heffalumping about it like anything.

"Oh, dear, oh, dear, oh, dear!" said Piglet to himself. And he wanted to run away. But somehow, having got so near, he felt that he must just see what a Heffalump was like. So he crept to the side of the Trap and looked in. . . .

And all the time Winnie-the-Pooh had been trying to get the honey-jar off his head. The more he shook it, the more tightly it stuck. "*Bother!*" he said, inside the jar, and "*Oh help!*" and, mostly, "*Ow!*" And he tried bumping it against things, but as he couldn't see what he was bumping it against, it didn't help him; and he tried to climb out of the Trap, but as he could see nothing but jar, and not much of that, he couldn't find his way. So at last he lifted up his head, jar and all, and made a loud, roaring noise of Sadness and Despair . . . and it was at that moment that Piglet looked down.

"Help, help!" cried Piglet, "a Heffalump, a Horrible Heffalump!" and he scampered off as hard as he could, still crying out,

"Help, help, a Herrible Hoffalump! Hoff, Hoff, a Hellible Horralump! Holl, Holl, a Hoffable Hellerump!" And he didn't stop crying and scampering until he got to Christopher Robin's house.

"Whatever's the matter, Piglet?" said Christopher Robin, who was just getting up.

"Heff," said Piglet, breathing so hard that he could hardly speak, "a Heff — a Heff — a Heffalump."

"Where?"

"Up there," said Piglet, waving his paw.

"What did it look like?"

"Like — like — It had the biggest head you ever saw, Christopher Robin. A great enormous thing, like — like

nothing. A huge big — well, like a — I don't know — like an enormous big nothing. Like a jar."

"Well," said Christopher Robin, putting on his shoes, "I shall go and look at it. Come on."

Piglet wasn't afraid if he had Christopher Robin with him, so off they went. . . .

"I can hear it, can't you?" said Piglet anxiously, as they got near.

"I can hear *something*," said Christopher Robin.

It was Pooh bumping his head against a tree-root he had found.

"There!" said Piglet. "Isn't it *awful*?" And he held on tight to Christopher Robin's hand.

Suddenly Christopher Robin began to laugh . . . and he laughed . . . and he laughed . . . and he laughed. And while he was still laughing — *Crash* went the Heffalump's head against the tree-root, Smash went the jar, and out came Pooh's head again. . . .

Then Piglet saw what a Foolish Piglet he had been, and he was so ashamed of himself that he ran straight off home and went to bed with a headache. But Christopher Robin and Pooh went home to breakfast together.

"Oh, Bear!" said Christopher Robin. "How I do love you!"

"So do I," said Pooh.

IN WHICH PIGLET IS ENTIRELY SURROUNDED BY WATER

It rained and it rained and it rained. Piglet told himself that never in all his life, and *he* was goodness knows *how* old — three, was it, or four? — never had he seen so much rain. Days and days and days.

"If only," he thought, as he looked out of the window, "I had been in Pooh's house, or Christopher Robin's house, or Rabbit's house when it began to rain, then I should have had Company all this time, instead of being here all alone, with nothing to do except wonder when it will stop." And he imagined himself with Pooh, saying, "Did you ever see such rain, Pooh?" and Pooh saying, "Isn't it *awful*, Piglet?" and Piglet saying, "I wonder how it is over Christopher Robin's way," and Pooh saying, "I should think poor old Rabbit is about flooded out by this time." It would have been jolly to talk like this, and really, it wasn't much good having anything exciting like floods, if you couldn't share them with somebody.

For it was rather exciting. The little dry ditches in which Piglet had nosed about so often had become streams, the little streams across which he had splashed were rivers, and the

river, between whose steep banks they had played so happily, had sprawled out of its own bed and was taking up so much room everywhere, that Piglet was beginning to wonder whether it would be coming into *his* bed soon.

"It's a little Anxious," he said to himself, "to be a Very Small Animal Entirely Surrounded by Water. Christopher Robin and Pooh could escape by Climbing Trees, and Kanga could escape by Jumping, and Rabbit could escape by Burrowing, and Owl could escape by Flying, and Eeyrore could escape by — by Making a Loud Noise Until Rescued, and here am I, surrounded by water and I can't do *anything.*"

It went on raining, and every day the water got a little higher, until now it was nearly up to Piglet's window . . . and still he hadn't done anything.

"There's Pooh," he thought to himself. "Pooh hasn't much Brain, but he never comes to any harm. He does silly things and they turn out right. There's Owl. Owl hasn't exactly got Brain, but he Knows Things. He would know the Right Thing to Do when Surrounded by Water. There's Rabbit. He hasn't Learnt in Books, but he can always Think of a Clever Plan. There's Kanga. She isn't Clever, Kanga isn't, but she would be so anxious about Roo that she would do a Good Thing to Do without thinking about it. And then there's Eeyore. And Eeyore is so miserable anyhow that he wouldn't mind about this. But I wonder what Christopher Robin would do?"

Then suddenly he remembered a story which Christopher Robin had told him about a man on a desert island who had written something in a bottle and thrown it into the sea; and Piglet thought that if he wrote something in a bottle and threw it in the water, perhaps somebody would come and rescue *him*!

He left the window and began to search his house, all of it that wasn't under water, and at last he found a pencil and a small piece of dry paper, and a bottle with a cork to it. And he wrote on one side of the paper:

HELP!
PIGLIT (ME)

and on the other side:

IT'S ME PIGLIT, HELP HELP!

Then he put the paper in the bottle, and he corked the bottle up as tightly as he could, and he leant out of his window as far as he could lean without falling in, and he threw the bottle as far as he could throw —

splash! — and in a little while it bobbed up again on the water; and he watched it floating slowly away in the distance, until his eyes ached with looking, and sometimes he thought it was the bottle, and sometimes he thought it was just a ripple on the water which he was following, and then suddenly he knew that he would never

see it again and that he had done all that he could do to save himself.

"So now," he thought, "somebody else will have to do something, and I hope they will do it soon, because if they don't I shall have to swim, which I can't, so I hope they do it soon." And then he gave a very long sigh and said, "I wish Pooh were here. It's so much more friendly with two."

. . . . . .

When the rain began Pooh was asleep. It rained, and it rained, and it rained, and he slept and he slept and he slept. He had had a tiring day. You remember how he discovered the North Pole; well, he was so proud of this that he asked Christopher Robin if there were any other Poles such as a Bear of Little Brain might discover.

"There's a South Pole," said Christopher Robin, "and I expect there's an East Pole and a West Pole, though people don't like talking about them."

Pooh was very excited when he heard this, and suggested that they should have an Expotition to discover the East Pole, but Christopher Robin had thought of something else to do with Kanga; so Pooh went out to discover the East Pole by himself. Whether he discovered it or not, I forget; but he was so tired when he got home that, in the very middle of his supper, after he had been eating for little more than half-an-

hour, he fell fast asleep in his chair, and slept and slept and slept.

Then suddenly he was dreaming. He was at the East Pole, and it was a very cold pole with the coldest sort of snow and ice all over it. He had found a beehive to sleep in, but there wasn't room for his legs, so he had left them outside. And Wild Woozles, such as inhabit the East Pole, came and nibbled all the fur off his legs to make Nests for their Young. And the more they nibbled, the colder his legs got, until suddenly he woke up with an *Ow!*— and there he was, sitting in his chair with his feet in the water, and water all round him!

He splashed to his door and looked out. . . .

"This is Serious," said Pooh. "I must have an Escape."

So he took his largest pot of honey and escaped with it to a broad branch of his tree, well above the water, and then he climbed down again and escaped with another pot . . . and when the whole Escape was finished, there was Pooh sitting on his branch, dangling his legs, and there, beside him, were ten pots of honey. . . .

Two days later, there was Pooh, sitting on his branch, dangling his legs, and there, beside him, were four pots of honey. . . .

Three days later there was Pooh, sitting on his branch, dangling his legs, and there beside him, was one pot of honey.

Four days later, there was Pooh . . .

And it was on the morning of the fourth day that Piglet's bottle came floating past him, and with one loud cry of "Honey!" Pooh plunged into the water, seized the bottle, and struggled back to his tree again.

"Bother!" said Pooh, as he opened it. "All that wet for nothing. What's that bit of paper doing?"

He took it out and looked at it.

"It's a Missage," he said to himself, "that's what it is. And that letter is a 'P', and so is that, and so is that, and 'P' means 'Pooh,' so it's a very important Missage to me, and I can't read it. I must find Christopher Robin or Owl or Piglet, one of those Clever Readers who can read things, and they will tell me what this missage means. Only I can't swim. Bother!"

Then he had an idea, and I think that for a Bear of Very Little Brain, it was a good idea. He said to himself:

"If a bottle can float, then a jar can float, and if a jar floats, I can sit on the top of it, if it's a very big jar."

So he took his biggest jar, and corked it up.

"All boats have to have a name," he said, "so I shall call mine *The Floating Bear.*" And with these words he dropped his boat into the water and jumped in after it.

For a little while Pooh and *The Floating Bear* were uncertain as to which of them was meant to be on the top, but after trying one or two different positions, they settled down with *The Floating Bear* underneath and Pooh triumphantly astride it, paddling vigorously with his feet.

• • • • • •

Christopher Robin lived at the very top of the Forest. It rained, and it rained, and it rained, but the water couldn't come up to *his* house. It was rather jolly to look down into the valleys and see the water all round him, but it rained so hard that he stayed indoors most of the time, and thought about things. Every morning he went out with his umbrella and put a stick in the place where the water came up to, and every next morning he went out and couldn't see his stick any more, so he put another stick in the place where the water came up to, and then he walked home again, and each morning he had a shorter way to walk than he had had the morning before. On the morning of the fifth day he saw the water all round him, and knew that for the first time in his life he was on a real island. Which was very exciting.

It was on this morning that Owl came flying over the water to say "How do you do?" to his friend Christopher Robin.

"I say, Owl," said Christopher Robin, "isn't this fun? I'm on an island!"

"The atmospheric conditions have been very unfavourable lately," said Owl.

"The what?"

"It has been raining," said Owl.

"Yes." said Christopher Robin. "It has."

"The flood-level has reached an unprecedented height."

"The who?"

"There's a lot of water about," explained Owl.

"Yes," said Christopher Robin, "there is."

"However, the prospects are rapidly becoming more favourable. At any moment —"

"Have you seen Pooh?"

"No. At any moment —"

"I hope he's all right," said Christopher Robin. "I've been wondering about him. I expect Piglet's with him. Do you think they're all right, Owl?"

"I expect so. You see, at any moment —"

"Do go and see, Owl. Because Pooh hasn't got very much brain, and he might do something silly, and I do love him so, Owl. Do you see, Owl?"

"That's all right," said Owl. "I'll go. Back directly." And he flew off.

In a little while he was back again.

"Pooh isn't there," he said.

"Not there?"

"He's *been* there. He's been sitting on a branch of his tree outside his house with nine pots of honey. But he isn't there now."

"Oh, Pooh!" cried Christopher Robin. "Where *are* you?"

"Here I am," said a growly voice behind him.

"Pooh!"

They rushed into each other's arms.

"How did you get here, Pooh?" asked Christopher Robin, when he was ready to talk again.

"On my boat," said Pooh proudly. "I had a Very Important Missage sent me in a bottle, and owing to having got some water in my eyes, I couldn't read it, so I brought it to you. On my boat."

With these proud words he gave Christopher Robin the missage.

"But it's from Piglet!" cried Christopher Robin when he had read it.

"Isn't there anything about Pooh in it?" asked Bear, looking over his shoulder.

Christopher Robin read the message aloud.

"Oh, are those 'P's' piglets? I thought they were poohs."

"We must rescue him at once! I thought he was with *you*, Pooh. Owl, could you rescue him on your back?"

"I don't think so," said Owl, after grave thought. "It is doubtful if the necessary dorsal muscles —"

"Then would you fly to him at *once* and say that Rescue is Coming? And Pooh and I will think of a Rescue and come as quick as ever we can. Oh, don't *talk*, Owl, go on quick?"
And, still thinking of something to say, Owl flew off.

"Now then, Pooh," said Christopher Robin, "where's your boat?"

"I ought to say," explained Pooh as they walked down to the shore of the island, "that it isn't just an ordinary sort of boat. Sometimes it's a Boat, and sometimes it's more of an Accident. It all depends."

"Depends on what?"

"On whether I'm on the top of it or underneath it."

"Oh! Well, where is it?"

"There!" said Pooh, pointing proudly to *The Floating Bear*.

It wasn't what Christopher Robin expected, and the more he looked at it, the more he thought what a Brave and Clever Bear Pooh was, and the more Christopher Robin thought this, the more Pooh looked modestly down his nose and tried to pretend he wasn't.

"But it's too small for two of us," said Christopher Robin sadly.

"Three of us with Piglet."

"That makes it smaller still. Oh, Pooh Bear, what shall we do?"

And then this Bear, Pooh Bear, Winnie-the-Pooh, F.O.P. (Friend of Piglet's), R.C. (Rabbit's Companion), P.D. (Pole Discoverer), E.C. and T.F. (Eeyore's Comforter and Tail-finder) — in fact, Pooh himself — said something so clever that Christopher Robin could only look at him with mouth open and eyes staring, wondering if this was really the Bear of Very Little Brain whom he had known and loved so long.

"We might go in your umbrella," said Pooh.

"?"

"We might go in your umbrella," said Pooh.

"??"

"We might go in your umbrella," said Pooh.

"!!!!!!"

For suddenly Christopher Robin saw that they might. He opened his umbrella and put it point downwards in the water. It floated but wobbled. Pooh got in. He was just beginning to say that it was all right now, when he found that it wasn't, so after a short drink, which he didn't really want, he waded back to Christopher Robin. Then they both got in together, and it wobbled no longer.

"I shall call this boat *The Brain of Pooh*," said Christopher Robin, and *The Brain of Pooh* set sail forthwith in a south-westerly direction, revolving gracefully.

You can imagine Piglet's joy when at last the ship came in sight of him. In after-years he liked to think that he had been

in Very Great Danger during the Terrible Flood, but the only danger he had really been in was the last half-hour of his imprisonment, when Owl, who had just flown up, sat on a branch of his tree to comfort him, and told him a very long story about an aunt who had once laid a seagull's egg by mistake, and the story went on and on, rather like this sentence, until Piglet who was listening out of his window without much hope, went to sleep quietly and naturally, slipping slowing out of the window towards the water until he was only hanging on by his toes, at which moment, luckily, a sudden loud squawk from Owl, which was really part of the story, being what his aunt said, woke the Piglet up and just gave him time to jerk himself back into safety and say, "How interesting, and did she?" when — well, you can imagine his joy when at last he saw the good ship, *Brain of Pooh* (*Captain*, C. Robin; 1*st Mate*, P. Bear) coming over the sea to rescue him. . . .

And as that is really the end of the story, and I am very tired after that last sentence, I think I shall stop there.

Happiness

John had
Great Big
Waterproof
Boots on;
John had a
Great Big
Waterproof
Hat;
John had a
Great Big
Waterproof
Mackintosh —
And that
(Said John)
Is
That.

The End

When I was One,
I had just begun.

When I was Two,
I was nearly new.

When I was Three,
I was hardly Me.

When I was Four,
I was not much more.

When I was Five,
I was just alive.

But now I am Six, I'm as clever as clever.
So I think I'll be six now for ever and ever.

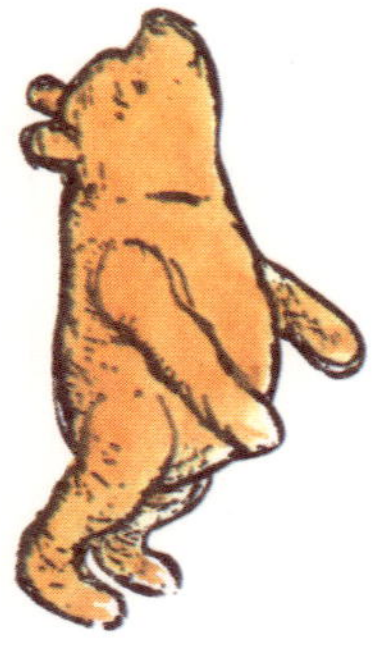

P
O
O
H
NICE FOR
KANGAS HOUSE
SANDY PIT WHERE ROO PLAYS
RABBITS HOUSE
POOH BEARS HOUSE
SIX PINE TREES
POOH TRAP FOR HEFFALUMPS
PIGLETS HOUSE
WHERE THE WOOZLE WASNT
FLOODY PLACE